Ali Alligator

A story of friendship

Dream Big Publishing

Ali Alligator

Cover: Jason DeGroff

Editor: Bernice Adcock Talent

Interior: Jonnie Kidd Whittington

Ali the alligator is born with three legs. This is a story of acceptance, friendship and forgiveness.

Library of Congress Cataloging-in-Publication Data

ISBN:

Ali Alligator

Dayla Ann Driver Daniels

Bernice Adcock Talent – Illustrator

1. Social skills 2. Friendship 3. Acceptance of others with disabilities 4. Forgiveness

---

Printed in the United States of America

There was once an alligator named Ali.

She had a mom and dad who loved her very much.

Ali was born with only three legs. They thought she was perfect.

One day her mom said, “Ali, it’s time you go out

and make some friends.”

Right away she rushed out of their pond to find some friends.

Ali went down a dirt path and saw a squirrel.

“What’s your name?” asked Ali. “Will you be my friend?”

“Oh my, an alligator!” screamed the squirrel.

Other animals panicked and ran away.

Ali didn’t mean to frighten them.

She was walking home . . . feeling so sad. Suddenly she came upon a baby deer . . . a spotted baby deer. The deer did not run. The deer said, “Hi, my name is Spots.”

Soon the other animals began to hang out with Ali, too.

She was so happy to have so many friends.

But then one day something happened.

Ali and Spots overheard their friends talking.

The cat and rabbit said, “We only hang out with Ali

because she has three legs.

The other animals replied, “Us, too. We feel sorry for her.”

Ali ran away and Spots ran after her.

Ali started to swim to her parents.

Spots followed after her . . .

even though she couldn’t swim.

When Ali told her mom and dad what happened,

her mom asked her who it was that had been so nice to her.

“It was Spots,” she said. “I am going to get her.”

Ali started to swim to shore when she saw something thrashing about in the water. Ali wanted to see what was causing all that splashing. When she got closer she saw it was Spots! Spots was in trouble!

Ali swam under Spots letting her ride on her back to shore.

"Wow! You are such a good friend!" Spots said.

"No," said Ali. "You are. Other than my family, you are the only one who likes me for who I really am."

Then Spots said, “I know what we have to do!”

This time Spots ran and Ali followed.

Then Spots began climbing the hill.

“Where are we going!” asked Ali.

“You will see,” said Spots.

"Everyone listen up!" Spots yelled. Everyone looked up at Spots.

"I am nice to Ali because she is a sweet alligator . . . NOT because she has three legs. I *like* her."

"We are sorry, Ali. We like you, too." said cat and rabbit.

"Us, too," the others replied.

Before she could say another word . . . Sammy Squirrel stepped up and said he was sorry for the time he screamed and scared everyone.

"That's okay," said Ali. "I forgive you."

Soon all the animals began to gather around Ali.

Some were slow but they all came around.

Everyone was her friend.

They played together all day.

After a long day of play, Ali finally went home to Mom and Dad.

She told them all the good news.

And they lived happily alligator after.

Alligator Facts and

Coloring Sheets of Ali and Friends

Alligator Facts:

Hi Kids, I hope you enjoyed the story, but alligators really are dangerous in
real life.

Please don't feed alligators because they will lose their fear of humans and
attack. Sorry if I scared you a little but they will.

Alligators live-in slow-moving water like ponds, lakes, and swamps.

Alligators are reptiles. They are cold blooded and because of that they cannot
keep themselves warm.

Alligators often bask in the sun so keep an eye out if you are around their
natural habitat.

Alligators can grow up to eleven feet and get up to one thousand pounds in
their weight.

Alligators are social creatures and like to live in groups called congregations.

Some tasty treats to alligators are birds, fish, turtles, and other things, but
hopefully not you.

In conclusion, kids, alligators are not pets. Please do not feed them and become their tasty treat.

Draw Ali on this page

Ali with her mom and dad

Draw Ali here

Good friends – Spots and Ali

Draw Ali here

Screaming squirrel was afraid of Ali

Draw Ali here

All of the animals decided to be Ali’s friend.

Draw Ali here

Ali, her mom and dad lived happily alligator ever after.

The End

Acknowledgements

A great big thank you to Writer's INK of Mayo FL, and my family for all of their encouragement and support on my first book. I love all of you!

Made in the USA
Columbia, SC
14 October 2018